I0694277

-

Contributing Author: Latoya Wakefield

Contributing Editors: Adam Davis, Erika Byers, David Berkshire, and Sherryce Robinson

Illustrations: Josh Brizuela

Narration (Audio Book): Albert Keronye

Background Score (Audio Book): Marion DeGuzman

-

To download the free audio book and e-book go to:

mojarobinson.com/hard-body

use code **"communitytool"**

-

Translations (Swahili):

**Dunia - Earth
Jua - Sun
Kichwa - Head
Maarifa - Knowledge
Mababu - Ancestors
Mdomo - Mouth
Moyo - Heart
Mwezi - Moon
Tumemaliza - Finished
Ukoloni - Colonialism
Umoja - Unity**

In loving memory of knowledge lost and stolen

The Sun and Moon Save Earth

by Maja Robinson

"Mwezi, Mama is calling us!"

Jua said to her brother.

Their mother, Dunia, was wheezing and had almost lost all the color she had. They missed their mother, who was once so green and filled with energy.

"Mama, Mama! What can we do to help?"

Mwezi cried out.

"Please, Mama, we will do anything to help you!"

Jua begged, smiling as she always did.

Jua believed that she had to shine bright for Mama, so she kept smiling even when she was afraid.

It broke Dunia's heart to see her children so sad. She
knew she needed to live on for them. So, she told
them about the only thing that could save her.

"Mwezi and Jua, follow the Mababu fireflies to the
forest. In the forest, you'll find the cure
for my sickness."

Mwezi and Jua kissed their dear mama on her
forehead, then began their mission to save her.

Upon entering the forest, they saw the most beautiful
fireflies. Together, they created a big ball of light.

"Those are the fireflies Mama said we should follow!"

"Let's go!"

They caught up to the fireflies and were led to Kichwa
Village. It wasn't as peaceful as they imagined it to be.
People were fighting and arguing.

"Give it to me! It's mine!"
"No, it's mine! I saw it first!"
"It does not matter, the plague has doomed us all!"

Jua and Mwezi were surprised that the village was
fighting over simple resources.

It seemed like the plague hurt so many people,
making life much harder, giving rise to selfishness.

WHOOSH!

Something flew through the ball of fireflies making
them scatter.

"No! Please come back!"

Jua shouted, but all the fireflies flew away.

"Let's go to that bridge!"

Jua urged Mwezi when she realized the fighting was getting out of control.

They hid under a Ukoloni forbidden bridge.

"Now, what do we do? We don't know the way?"

Jua pondered.

Mwezi looked around for a solution.

The Maarifa River underneath the bridge was like no other they had seen. It had a lot of junk in it and flies hovered above it, buzzing away. A green glow caught Mwezi's eye. It was right at the edge of the river.

"That looks like a...

"Mababu firefly!"

They didn't recognize it at first because its glow was different.

As if fueled by Mwezi's renewed hope, the firefly bolted out of the water and started moving away from the river.

"Let's go!", Jua advised.

They quickly and quietly followed the lone firefly
through a hole hidden under the bridge. Luckily,
none of the villagers who were fighting noticed.

They continued to follow the firefly through nooks
and crannies until they reached a sign that said

Mdomo Village.

When they finished reading the sign,
the firefly vanished.

They entered the village and noticed the villagers
looked thinner than the ones by the river, but there
was no fight or fury in their eyes.

The villagers told Jua and Mwezi they were fisher
folk and that the river was so polluted that they
could not fish anymore.

"Oh no!", Jua pleaded.

Mwezi told them about their sick mother and the
fighting they saw by the river.

"We know a forest that can save your mother
and we have a plant that cures the villager's plague,
but the Ukoloni has made the Umoja Bridge
forbidden and no one has returned from their
journey to that forest."

One of the villagers cautioned them.

Mwezi and Jua were determined, so they asked the
villagers to still show them the way to the forest.

"You can tell us!" Mwezi declared, holding Jua's hand.

They had to save their mother, no matter what it took.

The villagers directed them to Moyo Village,
where Ukoloni operated.

Jua and Mwezi thanked the fisher people.

As they walked away from the villagers, Jua began
to tremble.

"It'll be okay, sister..."

Mwezi expressed as they continued walking.

After an hour of walking, they saw a sign that read
"Ukoloni cures all illnesses and provides shelter for
anyone joining the Moyo Village."

"Let's pick up the pace!"

Jua shrilled at Mwezi as she sped ahead.

WOOOOOWWW!

At the entrance of the village, they saw dazzling
lights flashing different tones of purple.

"Mababu fireflies!"

They ran through the fireflies and the gate that
 led them to the Moyo Village.

"It's so beautiful!", Jua gasped.

BAM!

They turned around and saw that the gate had closed, and the fireflies started to fade.

"Let's continue?"

Mwezi mumbled hesitantly to Jua.

As they began walking, they noticed that the village had lost its color.

"Listen, the birds aren't chirping anymore."

The village changed in an instant.

Lively to lackluster, in a blink of an eye.

"It's okay, let's keep going."

Jua reassured Mwezi.

"Yeah, we have to."

Mwezi agreed.

"Ukoloni must be the source of the pollution"

Jua exposed to Mwezi.

As they ventured further into the soulless village, they saw some villagers and told them about what Ukoloni was doing.

The villagers looked at them with empty eyes,

"Why would the Ukoloni cause and relieve the sickness?"

One villager argued.

Then they faded away with the rest of the colorless village.

Mwezi looked at Jua.

"I'm okay."

she told him and walked on.

COLOR!

something said behind them.

"We have intruders!"

the shadow said.

It was Ukoloni!

"Run!" Jua screamed to Mwezi.

They dashed off as fast as lightning.

Suddenly, dozens of villagers blocked their path.

Jua and Mwezi tried pushing through the villagers, but more appeared.

"Grab them! We must take their color!"

Ukoloni demanded.

As Jua and Mwezi's color started to fully dissolve...

"Jua, look at the ground!"

She did and saw fireflies that were quickly disappearing, leading them to a path away from the crowd.

Jua grabbed Mwezi's hand, and they crawled out of the crowd.

Ukoloni tried to follow them, but the horde of villagers blocked the path.

Jua and Mwezi acrobatically pursued the fading
fireflies through the village onto the Ukoloni machine
causing it to explode!

The burst from the explosion catapulted Jua and
Mwezi over the Moyo Village borders into a forest
filled with Mababu fireflies of every color.

"No way, so many fireflies!"

Mwezi uttered as Jua paraded.

After some time, their excitement faded as the fireflies
weren't leading them anywhere.

They tried speaking to them about their sick mother
and the tragic villages, but the fireflies just buzzed on.

Feeling fatigued, hungry, and disappointed, Jua
and Mwezi rested on the ground and stared
at the radiant firefly-lit sky.

"My eyes feel heavy..." Jua nodded to Mwezi.

"Yeah, mine too, maybe we can take a little nap?"

As they closed their eyes, they heard

Ujamaa! Ujamaa! Ujamaa!

They got up slowly.

Jua yawned, as they sluggishly walked toward
the celebration.

It was the Mdomo Villagers celebrating on the
river, as it was no longer murky and smelly.
 It was beautiful and clean.

Jua and Mwezi couldn't believe it was the same river!

"Jua, Mwezi, join us!"

applauded the villagers when they saw them.

Mwezi and Jua joined the festivity, but they kept looking back at the forest, thinking of their mom.

They didn't stay with the villagers long.

"I think it's time we go back home?"

Mwezi cooed.

"Don't worry, we'll take you home!"

The villagers boasted.

Jua and Mwezi politely thanked them.

During their journey back, they saw the soulless village popping with color and musical vibrations.

UKOLONI WAS GONE.

Nearing home, the Kichwa villagers joined them on
the boat and told them that the Mdomo and Kichwa
united to fight the plague and to grow the
fishing ecosystem.

"We promise to always look out for our people. No
Ukoloni will get between us again!"

The villagers claimed.

They took Jua and Mwezi all the way to the forbidden
Umoja Bridge.

"You can cross now. It's finally safe."

Although Mwezi and Jua were happy for the villagers,
they were also sad.

They thanked the villagers and began making their
way home.

"What do we tell mom?"

Jua asked.

Mwezi didn't say anything at first.

"Let's just tell her we tried and that we love her."

Jua agreed as they began reflecting on their long and disappointing journey.

"Did we miss something?"

Mwezi muttered as tears ran down his face.

"It'll be alright, brother!"

Jua soothed with a hug.

Mwezi wasn't sure it would be, but he nodded his
head to not scare his sister.

They kept walking until they saw their home.

"Something has changed?"

Jua blurted, squinting her eyes to see what was
happening at their home.

There were all sorts of colors flying
above their home.

It was...

"Mababu!" Jua and Mwezi shouted as they sprinted toward their door.

A huge smile arose on their faces as they saw who was full of life waiting for them at the door.

Tumemaliza

Symbolism

The Sun and Moon Save Earth symbolizes how colonialism dictates our environmental crisis and its effect on social classes. Colonialism (Ukoloni) is used in place of Colonists (Mkoloni) to emphasize that our modern issues are systemic and can not be relieved by having or removing one specific person as a leader. This dilemma is highlighted in America with Post-Obama and Post-Trump Syndrome. The Kichwa Village represents how colonialism affects our minds, the Mdomo Village illustrates how colonialism affects our bodies, and the Moyo Village portrays how colonialism affects our souls. The Mababu Fireflies personify our ancestors and ancestors' wisdom to remedy the villages' troubles. The blue ancestors underscore peace, unity, and conservatism. The green ancestors accentuate health, growth, and nature, and the purple ancestors embody spirituality, transformation, and enlightenment. The pollution of the Maarifa River and the blocking of the Umoja Bridge demonstrates how colonialism, governments, and its derivatives have historically dismembered parties, prevented unifications, and restricted or destroyed knowledge. Jua and Mwezi's interactions with these beings stress why interdependence, intersectionality, and indigenous knowledge must lead the Just Transition. The children's faces are kept indistinct to express that their acts of bravery and equity can be mirrored by any one of us.

Recommended Reads

Braiding Sweetgrass by Robin Wall Kimmerer

Climate Justice by Mary Robinson

Indigenous Research Methodologies by
Bagele Chilisa

Let My People Go Surfing by Yvon Chouinard

Tentacle by Rita Indiana

The Intersectional Environmentalist by Leah Thomas

The Responsibility Revolution by
Jeffrey Hollender & Bill Breen

The World We Need by Audrea Lim

What a Plant Knows by Daniel Chamovitz

The Sun and Moon Save Earth

Two siblings are on a quest, guided by their ancestors to save their
mother. On their path, they face tribal warfare, famine, and a soulless
society. The only way to complete their journey is to figure out how
these issues are interconnected.

Throughout the story, Robinson highlights the Swahili language
and Bantu worldview to spotlight three concepts:

(1) we have to fix ourselves, mind, body, and soul before we
can fix the earth

(2) doing this will help us relearn that non-human, living, and
non-living beings are equal to humans, and

(3) solutions only come when root issues are centered.

The fundamental concepts of The Sun and Moon Save Earth derive
from Moja Robinson's thesis paper, Corporate Social Responsibility
Upholds Colonialism — So What Now?. In addition, The Sun and
Moon Save Earth is part of a multimedia series by Robinson. Both
can be explored at **mojarobinson.com/hard-body**

About the Author

Moja is at the nexus of multidisciplinary
design and socio-environmental justice.
Moja's mission is to evolve business culture
to encompass equitable and regenerative
relationships and practices with the
environment and marginalized groups.